cloverleaf books™

Fall and Winter Holidays

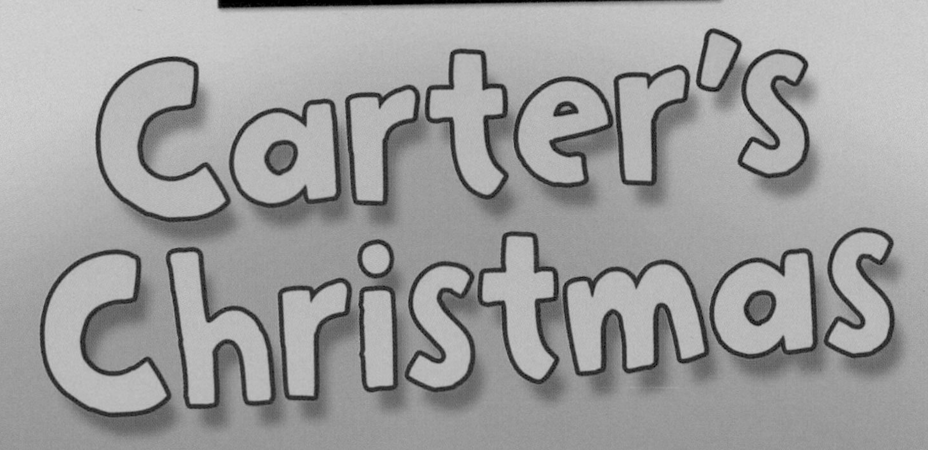

Carter's Christmas

Lisa Bullard

illustrated by Katie Saunders

MILLBROOK PRESS · MINNEAPOLIS

For Alex —L.B.

For my nephews William and Ned —K.S.

Millbrook Press
A division of Lerner Publishing Group, Inc.
241 First Avenue North
Minneapolis, MN 55401 U.S.A.

Website address: www.lernerbooks.com

Main body text set in Slappy Inline 18/28.
Typeface provided by T26.

Library of Congress Cataloging-in-Publication Data

Bullard, Lisa.
Carter's Christmas / by Lisa Bullard ; illustrated by Katie Saunders.
p. cm. — (Cloverleaf books. Fall and winter holidays)
Includes index.
ISBN 978-0-7613-5074-3 (lib. bdg. : alk. paper)
1. Christmas—Juvenile literature. I. Saunders, Katie, ill. II. Title.
GT4985.5.B86 2013
394.2663—dc23 2011046172

Manufactured in the United States of America
1 - BP - 7/15/12

TABLE OF CONTENTS

Chapter One

Christmas Is Coming

Ho, ho, ho! My name is Carter. I'm making an **ornament** for Grandma.

It's her **Christmas** present. But I'm having trouble keeping it a secret. Uh-oh! Here she comes!

Many people around the world celebrate Christmas on December 25.

Grandma says it's time to go Christmas shopping. We need to find **gifts** for everyone on our list.

LINE STARTS HERE

I get to see Santa Claus at the mall too!

Many children tell Santa what they want for Christmas. Some visit him at stores. Others write letters and mail them to the North Pole.

On the way home, we stop to buy our Christmas tree. Grandma asks me to help her decorate it right away.

Long ago, people in Europe decorated their homes with evergreens. In Germany, evergreen trees became popular at Christmas. Some Germans came to the United States. They brought the idea of Christmas trees with them.

You know how grown-ups are! They just can't wait for anything. But when will I work on her present?

Chapter Two
Christmas Tastes Great

It's **Christmas Eve**. I'm still not done with the ornament. But I can't work on it now!

We're **decorating cookies** with our neighbors. The cookies are shaped like things that make us think of Christmas.

Different things stand for Christmas in different places. In India, people decorate banana trees instead of pine trees. In Australia, some people picture kangaroos pulling Santa's sleigh.

Chapter Three

The Christmas Story

We go to church that night. We sing **carols.**

The pastor tells the **Christmas story**. It's about Jesus being born long ago. Grandma says Jesus was the first Christmas present!

Jesus was born about two thousand years ago. It was in the country now called Israel. Some people came to believe Jesus was the son of God. They started a new religion called Christianity. Later, Christians began celebrating December 25 as Jesus's birthday. It became a holiday.

Jesus's mother was Mary. She was engaged to marry Joseph. They were traveling when Jesus was born.

Christmas is a church holiday for some people. But not only Christians celebrate Christmas. It's a special day for many people. They celebrate being with family. They give one another gifts.

They didn't have a bed for Jesus. He had to sleep in a **manger!** That's a box that holds animal food.

After church, we tell everyone **Merry Christmas!** Then we drive by lots of houses decorated with lights.

December days are very dark. People celebrated this dark time of year long before Christmas. They were happy that soon the sun would rise earlier and set later. People now often put up colorful lights for Christmas.

Chapter Four

Present Time

Finally, I hear Grandma snoring. I sneak out to the kitchen. It's time to finish that ornament!

Cookies

A man called Saint Nicholas lived 1,700 years ago. He loved children and gave people gifts. Over time, Saint Nicholas became known as Santa Claus in some places. At Christmas, some children hang stockings. They hope Santa will fill the stockings with presents.

I listen for **Santa** while I work. He'll be here soon to fill my stocking. I hope he doesn't care that I'm eating his cookies.

Lots of relatives come over on Christmas. We eat tasty food and open presents. I get the biggest present of all.

In the United States, Christmas is a fun time for children and families. But that wasn't always true. The change happened in the 1800s. Several authors wrote stories or poems about Christmas. They helped make Christmas a children's holiday.

But Grandma says that she got the **best present!**

Make Your Own Ornament

What you will need:

A plastic lid, such as those from a potato chip can (to make a small ornament) or a coffee can (to make a large ornament)
A hole punch
Christmas ribbon
Christmas wrapping paper
Your school photo (in a size that fits your lid)
White construction paper
Colored markers
Scissors
Glue stick
Optional: glitter, sequins, confetti, colored buttons

Make your ornament:

1) Make sure your plastic lid is clean and dry.
2) Lay the lid on the back side of the Christmas wrapping paper. Trace around the lid with a marker, forming a circle.
3) Cut out the wrapping paper circle.
4) Lay the lid on the white construction paper. Trace around the lid with a marker, forming a circle.
5) Cut out the construction paper circle.
6) Use your colored markers to decorate the construction paper circle. Here are some ideas:
    draw a Christmas picture
    write your name and the year
    write something like, "Merry Christmas, Grandma"
7) Use your glue stick to glue the decorated circle to one side of your plastic lid. This will be the back.
8) Glue the Christmas paper circle to the other side of your lid. This will be the front. Make sure that the pretty side is facing out.
9) Glue your school photo on top of the Christmas paper.
10) If desired, decorate with glitter, sequins, confetti, or colored buttons.
11) Use the hole punch to punch a hole near the top of the ornament.
12) Thread the Christmas ribbon through the hole, and then tie it for a hanger.

GLOSSARY

carols: songs about Christmas

celebrate: do something to show how special or important something is

Christianity: a religion that follows the life and teachings of Jesus

decorate: add things to something to make it look pretty

evergreens: plants or trees that stay green all year long

manger: an open box where food for animals such as horses or cows is placed

ornament: a thing that decorates something else. Ornaments are small items that hang from the branches of Christmas trees.

pastor: the person who leads a church

religion: a set of beliefs in a god or gods

Ornament Front

Ornament Back

TO LEARN MORE

BOOKS

Heiligman, Deborah. *Celebrate Christmas: With Carols, Presents, and Peace.* Washington, DC: National Geographic, 2007.
Read more about the history of Christmas and how it is celebrated around the world.

Moore, Clement C. *The Night Before Christmas.* Kennebunkport, ME: Applesauce Press, 2011.
This picture book presents a classic story about Christmas and Santa along with beautiful illustrations.

Pienkowski, Jan. *The First Christmas.* New York: Knopf, 2011.
This book tells the story of the baby Jesus's birth on the first Christmas.

WEBSITES

N.J. Christmas Tree Activity Guide and Fun Book
http://www.njchristmastrees.org/f/ActivityGuidepdf.pdf
Download and print this guide from the New Jersey Christmas Tree Growers Association. It has many activities to help you learn more about Christmas trees.

Santa's Little Helper
http://learnenglishkids.britishcouncil.org/en/short-stories/santas-little-helper
Visit this website from the British Council to read a story about a girl named Amy who helps Santa deliver the Christmas presents.

LERNER e SOURCE™
Expand learning beyond the printed book. Download free, complementary educational resources for this book from our website, www.lerneresource.com.